W9-AFN-326

AUG 2 6 2010
Northville District Library
212 W. Cady Street
Northville, MI 48167-1560

READY TO BRAWL

VEXOS VS. RESISTANCE

GUIDEBOOK

by Tracey West

SCHOLASTIC INC.
NEW YORK TORONTO LONDON AUCKLAND
SYDNEY MEXICO CITY NEW DELHI HONG KONG

ISBN: 978-0-545-15522-9

12 11 10 9 8 7 6 5 4 3 2 1 10 11 12 13 14 15/0
Printed in the U.S.A. 40
First printing, January 2010

Meet the New Bakugan!

After Dan, Wavern, and Drago saved Vestroia from destruction, the Bakugan world transformed into a paradise: New Vestroia. The Bakugan who had been stranded on Earth returned to their home to live in their true forms, in peace.

But that peace didn't last long. The Vestals invaded New Vestroia, looking for some extra space for their overcrowded planet. At first they didn't realize that Bakugan were intelligent beings. They enslaved them and forced them to battle one another for sport.

Dan's old friend Drago returned to Earth and brought Dan and Marucho to New Vestroia to help free the Bakugan. They quickly met up with Mira, Ace, and Baron, three brawlers who fought for the Resistance.

Dan's new battles began right away, and each time he encountered new brawlers, new rules—and plenty of new Bakugan. In this mini guide, you'll meet some of the Bakugan from New Vestroia. Some are fast, some are tough, and some are mean—but they're all waiting for the chance to battle a brawler just like you!

ALTAIR

Looks Like: A large mechanical dragon with a long, curved tail and gleaming metal horns.

Battle Style: Altair attacks with its sharp-as-swords fangs and horns while it blasts out white-hot steam from its mouth.

Where You've Seen It: Lync uses a Ventos Altair to battle against the Bakugan Brawler Resistance.

BALITON

Looks Like: A monster with a protective shell on his back. Baliton has large spikes along his head, shell, and tail.

Battle Style: Baliton can swing his long tail like a baseball bat.

Where You've Seen Him: Mira used Baliton to strengthen her attack against Altair when Lync first battled with the mechanical beast.

BRONTES

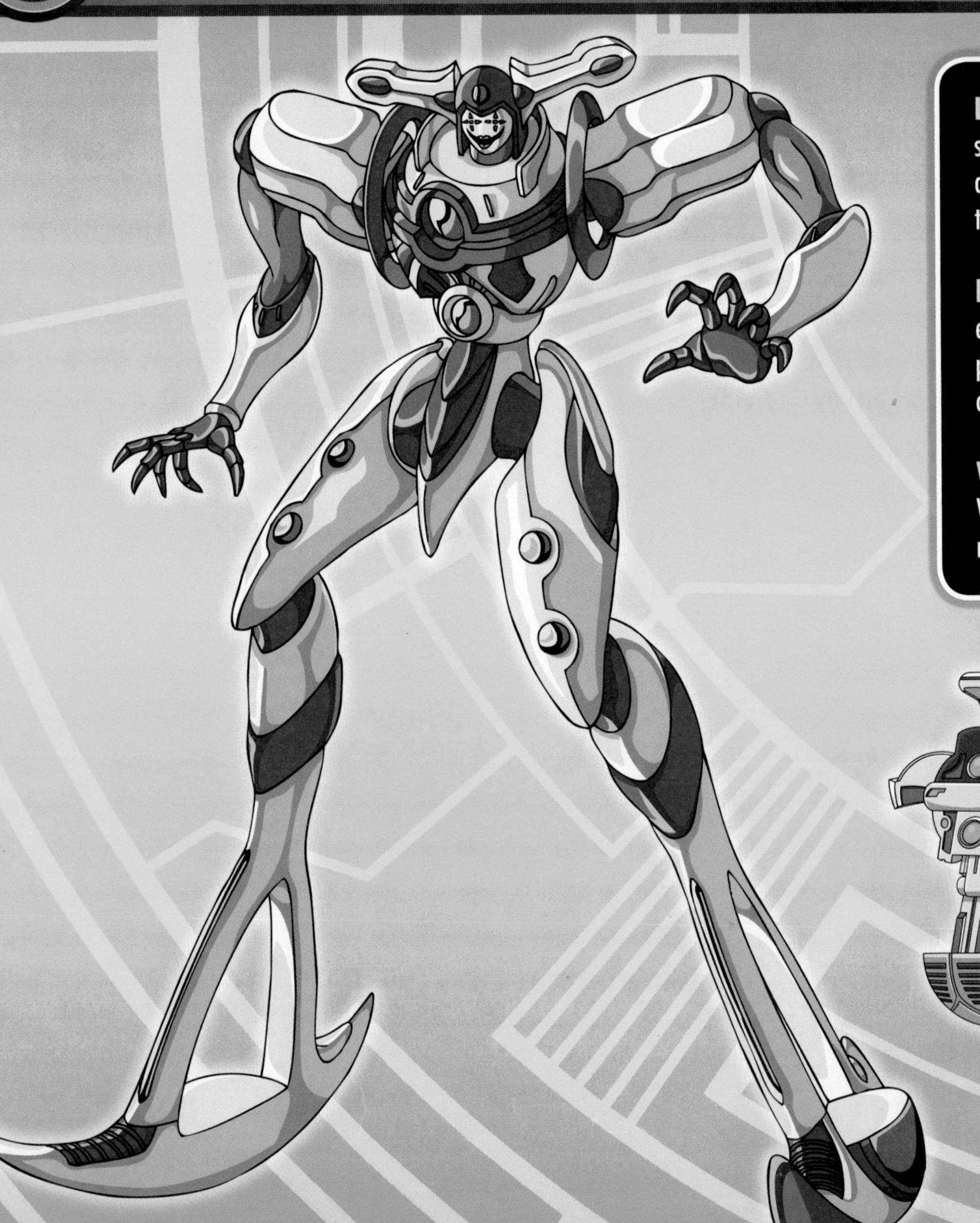

Looks Like: A long and slender robot with eight arms sticking out of its head that act as a propeller.

Battle Style: Brontes eliminates its rivals by wrapping its long arms around its opponents.

Where You've Seen It: Volt, a Vexos warrior, is partnered with a Haos Brontes.

DYNAMO

Looks Like: A six-legged robotic insect.

Battle Style: Dynamo uses its pincers to grab opponents.

Where You've Seen It: After saving Marucho from some quicksand, Volt challenged him—and used this Bakugan trap to secure his victory.

ELFIN

Looks Like: A cross between a frog and a fairy with a long tail, winglike flippers, and webbed hands and feet.

Battle Style: Elfin loves to turn the tables on her opponents with a quick attribute change.

Where You've Seen Her: While searching the woods of New Vestroia, Marucho encountered Elfin. She refused to join him at first, but changed her mind when Mylene showed up to steal the Bakugan in her forest. Elfin and Marucho have been brawling together ever since.

ELICO

Looks Like: A bulky robot with the face of a human, and clawed, animal-like feet.

Battle Style: Elico shoots a powerful blast of water from the golden diamond on his chest to defeat his opponents.

Where You've Seen Him: Although Mylene of Vexos chooses to brawl with brains instead of power, she often relies upon her Bakugan Elico and his brute strength.

FALCON FLY

Looks Like: A giant dragonfly.

Battle Style: The super-vibrations from Falcon Fly's powerful wings are strong enough to destroy buildings. Enemies don't stand a chance.

Where You've Seen It: When Ace and Shun battled Volt and Lync at the Alpha City Stadium, Ace used Falcon Fly to boost Percival's chances.

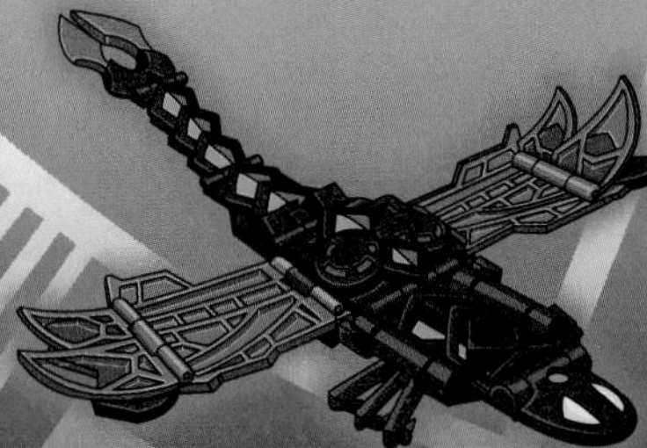

FORTRESS

Looks Like: A huge robot with ten cannons sticking out from his arms and legs.

Battle Style: Fortress can fly thanks to the rockets under his feet. He uses these to avoid enemy fire.

Where You've Seen Him: Shadow used Fortress in combination with Hades to defeat Shun in a one-on-one match.

New Vestroia, New Rules

When Dan came to New Vestroia, he had to learn how to do things in a whole new way. Good thing Dan is a fast learner—at least, with Bakugan, anyway.

Gotta Have a Gauntlet

In New Vestroia, you can't battle without a gauntlet. You strap it to your arm just like a Bakugan Shooter, but a gauntlet's different. If you load a Bakugan ball onto the gauntlet, the gauntlet will download its stats that you can read on a screen. You can use your gauntlet to load Ability Cards, too. But maybe the most important part of the gauntlet is the life gauge on the side. As a brawler's Bakugan loses battles, the life gauge goes down. The battle's over when one brawler's life gauge reaches zero. It's a clear way to determine the winner.

HADES

Looks Like: A mechanical, mythical monster with three heads, three tails, and six wings.

Battle Style: Hades attacks opponents from many different directions using the spiked tip on the end of each of his tails.

Where You've Seen Him: Shadow is the number one Darkus brawler in New Vestroia. So it's fitting that his main Bakugan is named after an ancient lord of the underworld.

HELIOS

Looks Like: A huge, powerful dragon with large wings and a long tail that ends in a curved blade.

Battle Style: Attack Viper Helios, and you'll have to dodge a red-hot fire blast shot from his mouth.

Where You've Seen Him: Spectra used Helios to battle Dan and Drago. Spectra didn't unleash the Bakugan's full power in that battle, because he wanted to see exactly what Drago could do.

INGRAM

Looks Like: A cross between an angel and a bird of prey.

Battle Style: When Ingram evolved from Cosmic Ingram, it grew more wings so it could fly faster; its eyes can see Bakugan from miles away; and metal plates protect its body in battle.

Where You've Seen It: Ingram battles with Shun the way his former Bakugan, Skyress, used to.

METALFENCER

Looks Like: A robot with clawed feet and cannons on the ends of its arms.

Battle Style: This Trap Bakugan can quickly move around the battlefield on its four legs, and can send a laser blast from its tail.

Where You've Seen It: Spectra used Metalfencer in a battle with Dan. He combined Metalfencer with Helios using Battle Unit Mode—making for a challenging battle.

Looks Like: An Egyptian king in gold and blue armor.

Battle Style: Nemus uses its wrist guards to deflect attacks.

Where You've Seen It: When Vexos Shadow came around looking for a brawl, Baron and his Haos Nemus stood up to Shadow and won the battle.

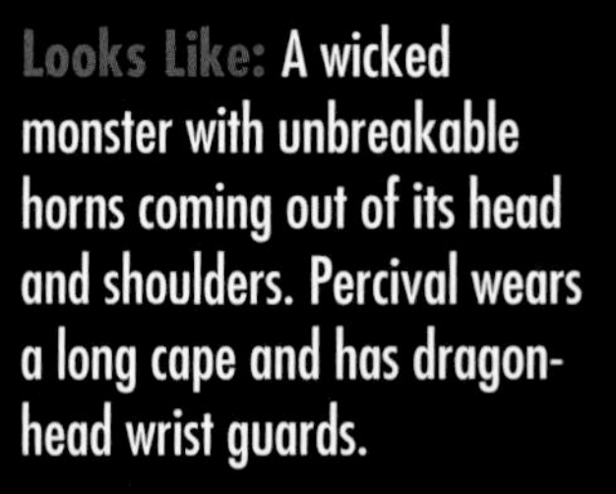

Looks Like: A wicked monster with unbreakable horns coming out of its head and shoulders. Percival wears a long cape and has dragon-head wrist guards.

Battle Style: It can shoot plasma bullets from its three mouths and take down challengers with a black tornado burning with purple sparks.

Where You've Seen It: Resistance member Ace uses a Darkus Percival in battle.

PIERCIAN

Looks Like: A giant robot made of metal blocks.

Battle Style: This Bakugan Trap has huge shields that can become bigger to boost his defensive ability in battle.

Where You've Seen Him: When Baron faced Lync, he combined the powers of Nemus and Piercian to send Lync's metal beasts to the junkyard.

PREMO VULCAN

Looks Like: A massive metal Viking warrior with curved horns coming out of its head.

Battle Style: Premo Vulcan has rocket launchers built into its feet so it can fly, which allows it to avoid blows as well as deliver more powerful attacks.

Where You've Seen It: When number-two ranked Vexos brawler Gus joined up with Spectra, he set his sights on Dan and Drago with his Premo Vulcan alongside him.

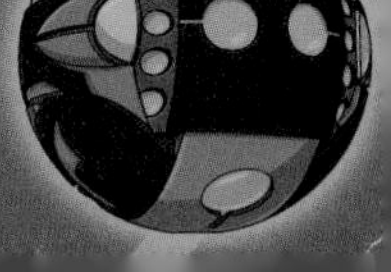

TRIPOD EPSILON

Looks Like: A frog, but not a typical one. Tripod Epsilon is big!

Battle Style: Powerful leaps, camouflage, and eyes that can control opponents' actions are all skills this Bakugan uses in battle.

Where You've Seen Him: When Marucho battled Lync in the desert, he used Tripod Epsilon and Elfin.

WILDA

Looks Like: A massive collection of boulders with arms and legs.

Battle Style: Wilda uses her powerful body to pound the ground and shake up her opponents before finishing them with a karate chop.

Where You've Seen Her: The first time Dan and Marucho met Mira they were amazed when she activated two abilities at the same time while brawling with Wilda.

WIRED

Looks Like: A bird's beak, with two razor-sharp wings.

Battle Style: Wired's sharp talons can shred almost any foe.

Where You've Seen Him: When Shun and Ace faced Lync and Volt in a double battle, Lync combined Altair with Wired, but it wasn't enough to defeat the Bakugan Battle Brawlers!